D0516275

SHE
LEADS
The Elephant
Matriarch

Library of Congress Control Number:

2019956688

Print ISBN 9781641702324

Ebook ISBN 9781641702973

Printed in China

Edited by Lacey Wulf

Cover & jacket design by Carlos Guerrero

Illustrations by Yumi Shimokawara

1098765432

First Edition

SHE LEADS
The Elephant Matriarch

June Smalls

For my daughter, and her daughters,
their daughters and their daughters...

Illustrations by Yumi Shimokawara

She is the queen. The matriarch.

A matriarchal society is a group or family led by a female. The head female is known as the matriarch. She is usually the oldest, but not always. It is her job to guide and teach her subjects to give them the best opportunities for survival. Female elephants are known as *cows*.

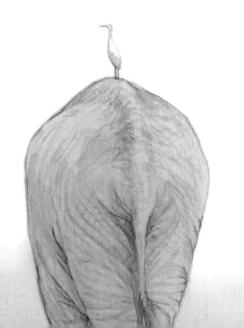

She leads her daughters and their daughters.

Elephants tend to stay with their blood relatives. This means many generations of the same family live together in the family unit or group. If the group gets too large, it may split into smaller groups. Males are called *bulls* and leave the group around age 13.

She shows them where to find food . . .

Elephants travel miles each day foraging for food. Elephants eat grasses, bushes, bark, and roots. In one day, an adult elephant can consume up to 300 pounds of food. If food is scarce, they will walk up to 50 miles to find a new food source.

. . . and water.

Water is vital to survival. An elephant drinks 40 to 60 gallons each day. At watering holes, they cover themselves in mud to protect their skin from the sun and from insects.

Knowledge, such as the location of watering holes, is passed down from elephant to elephant from past generations. During the dry season, they will dig into dry streambeds to uncover the water hiding beneath the surface. They use their feet, tusks, and trunks. This helps not only their group, but also other animals that then use this new watering hole.

When the rain doesn't fall, she guides them on journeys to watering holes remembered from long ago.

She teaches them
how to care for
the young.

Mothers are pregnant for 22 months. Older elephants help new mothers when they give birth. Grandmothers, aunts, and sisters help rear the young. The clumsy babies are sometimes caught in mud or water and the older elephants will work together to push, pull, or dig to rescue them.

And who their friends are.

Sometimes those groups that had split apart will meet in the same areas and forage for food together. These meetings are like a family reunion. Everyone goes back with their own group when they leave.

If elephants sense danger, such as hearing a lion roar, the group will huddle around the matriarch and other older females to see how they handle the situation. Babies are placed in the center of the huddle for protection. If there is a close threat, the elephants might charge. They will stomp or use their tusks as weapons.

When danger arrives,
she protects and stands strong against threats.

If nature or predators or poachers
take her friends, she will comfort
and care for the orphans.

An elephant calf is vitally dependent on their mother's milk until they are about two
years old. If they are orphaned prior to age two, their odds of survival are poor.
After age two, they may team up with other orphans or be adopted by other elephants.
Grandmothers or older siblings are the most likely to adopt the orphans.

She watches over the family
as they play and grow.

Elephant calves sometimes play by rubbing, bumping, or even climb-ing on one another. They play with toys such as logs, sticks, and grass. When mud isn't available, dust baths will have to do.

She teaches her children and their children
and their children so that when she is gone,
another matriarch will lead her family.

Elephants are not born with all the skills they need. They learn them from their elders. This includes interacting with other elephants, foraging, and safety. The baby elephants copy the older elephants in the group.

When the calf is born, it doesn't know how to use its trunk. Like a human child's hands, it takes practice to pick things up and move them. The elephant's trunk has about 100,000 muscles. They have the strength to move logs and still have the ability to gently pluck a leaf from a tree.

A princess becomes the queen. The matriarch.

Elephants can live up to 70 years in the wild. Elephants have been observed burying their dead with grasses and branches. They will sometimes stay with the dead for a few days. They will return months later and touch the bones of their lost family member. When the matriarch dies, the whole group changes. One female, usually the oldest daughter of the matriarch, will take charge.

She calls to her daughters
and their daughters.

Elephants can communicate over long distances. While we can hear their trumpets and their rumbles, they also make sounds too low for humans to hear. Sounds travel farther in the cool night air. In the best conditions, their sounds can travel 110 square miles. This ability to communicate is an important survival skill.

Open your eyes, princess.
One day you will lead.

When a baby is born, the group will circle the mother and baby to protect
them from predators. They nudge and lift the defenseless baby
to encourage her to stand and drink.

BBC. "Baby Elephant Gets Stuck in the Mud - Natural World 2016: Preview - BBC Two," YouTube, posted May 11, 2016, https://www.youtube.com/watch?v=18srVaQwwjg

BBC Earth. "Elephant Matriarch Shows Kindness to Orphans," *This Wild Life*, YouTube, posted October 6, 2016, https://www.youtube.com/watch?v=nK7n1EqX1NQ

Bekoff, Marc. "In Elephant Society, Matriarchs Lead," Live Science, posted January 15, 2014, www.livescience.com/42576-elephant-matriarchs-guide-society.html.

"Crack the Code of Elephant Communication," *Unforgettable Elephants*, PBS Nature, posted October 14, 2008, www.pbs.org/wnet/nature/unforgettable-elephants-crack-the-code-of-elephant-communication/5885/.

"Elephants." Defenders of Wildlife, accessed September 19, 2016, defenders.org/elephants.

Fishlock, Vicki. "Why Matriarchs Matter in Elephant Society," International Fund for Animal Welfare, posted June 9, 2011, www.ifaw.org/united-states/node/2842. (Page discontinued.)

Kiss, Gabriella. "Elephants Dig for Water," Africa Geographic, posted May 30, 2016, africageographic.com/blog/elephants-dig-water/.

Meyer, Amelia. "Elephants Communication," *Elephants Forever*, posted 2015, www.elephantsforever.co.za/elephant-communication.html.

National Geographic Society. "Elephants." *National Geographic*, www.nationalgeographic.org/topics/elephants/.

Ogden, Lesley Evans. "What Elephants Can Teach Us about the Importance of Female Leadership." *The Washington Post*, posted January 27, 2014, https://www.washingtonpost.com/national/health-science/what-elephants-can-teach-us-about-the-importance-of-female-leadership/2014/01/27/32db3f5e-7eeb-11e3-95c6-0a7aa80874bc_story.html.

Quarters, Cindy. "How Do Elephants Get Water During the Dry Season?" Pets on Mom.com, posted November 21, 2017, animals.mom.me/elephants-water-during-dry-season-3322.html.

Williams, Helena. "Six Facts about Elephant Families." *The Independent*, posted December 19, 2013, www.independent.co.uk/voices/comment/six-facts-about-elephant-families-9015298.html.

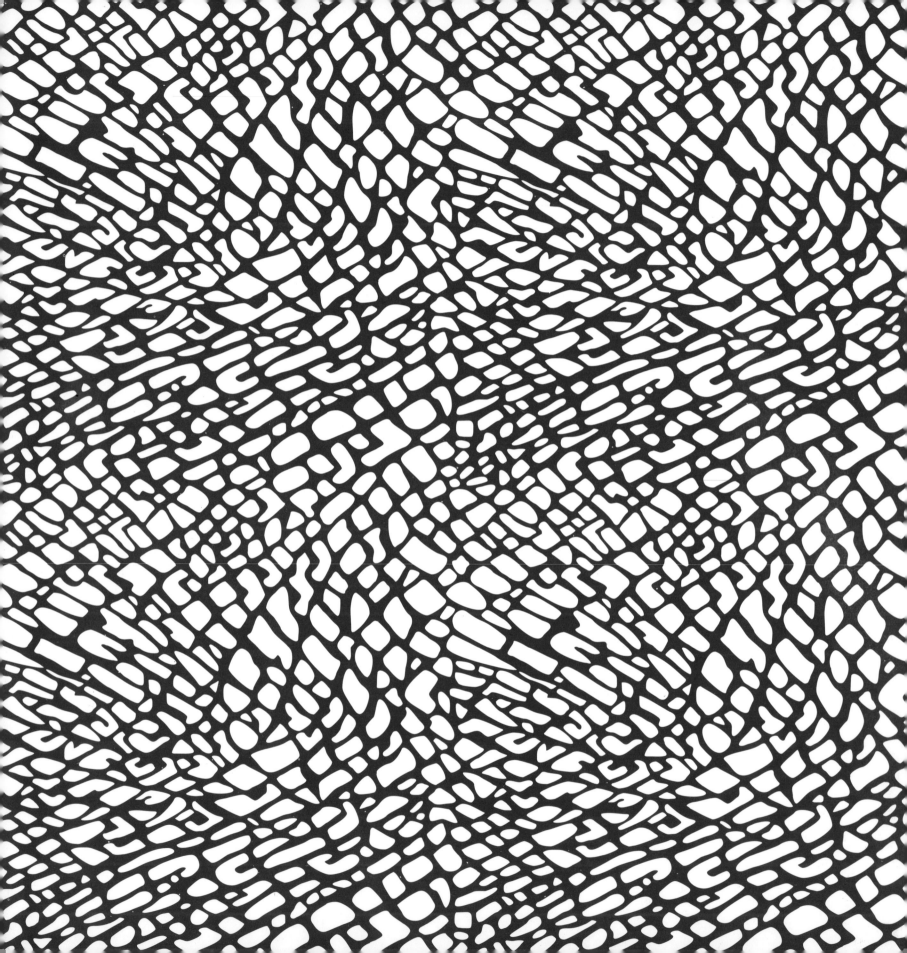